The Shadowmaker

THE $\mathscr{S}HADOWMAKER$

by Ron Hansen · illustrations by Margot Tomes

HarperTrophy
A Division of HarperCollinsPublishers

Library of Congress Cataloging-in-Publication Data
Hansen, Ron, 1947-
    The shadowmaker.

    Summary: A cunning little girl named Drizzle
rescues her town from the bedlam created by the
mysterious Shadowmaker, a wizard who makes new
shadows for people.
    [1. Wizards—Fiction.   2. Shadows—Fiction]
I. Tomes, Margot, ill.   II. Title.
PZ7.H198256Sh 1987   [Fic]   85-45272
ISBN 0-06-022202-6
ISBN 0-06-022203-4 (lib. bdg.)   j Fic

    (A Harper Trophy book)
ISBN 0-06-440287-8 (pbk.)

First Harper Trophy edition, 1989.

for Diane, Kirsten, Mary Pat, Nikki,
Rebecca, and Christianna

The Shadowmaker

1

ONCE upon a time, in a place you've never been, there was a town where nearly everyone was completely happy. Then along came a little man whom no one knew, riding on a big red coach that was like nothing anyone had ever seen before. The coach was pulled by a giant white horse that was so drowsy, the little man clanged together two garbage can lids in order to keep it awake.

The little man was so short he could stand upright beneath a kitchen sink. His voice was high and squawky, like a duck's might be if you stepped on its foot. He wore a gray bowler hat, large rubber boots, and a blue greatcoat that dragged on the ground when he walked. His hair and mustache and vast beard were white, and his eyebrows were black briers that shaded his cheeks like awnings. As the little man scuttled from store to store, poking about and handling things and asking all sorts of questions, he constantly tinkered with a crooked pipe that burned out inside of a minute.

"I'm a shopkeeper," the little man said. "Or at least I hope to be one. Could you give me the scoop on this place?"

"The scoop?" asked a plumber.

"You know, Are the people rich? Are they pleased with themselves? Is there anything you need here?"

"Haven't you heard?" the plumber said. "There's nothing we need. We have everything. We're all completely happy. Any fool can see that."

"Gotcha," the little man said, and winking

with pleasure he tipped his gray bowler hat in good-bye.

Over the next few days the little man was seen scurrying this way and that. There was a lot of gossip about him. People said that he was buying cans of black paint and measuring people with a tape and that he was renting a shop next to the bakery. One boy reported that he'd seen the little man back up the red coach to the shop's loading dock and drag out a big, black trunk that was chained and padlocked shut. A girl said she'd gone past the little man's shop one night and heard him "banging things." Then no one saw the little man or heard him for more than a week. In fact, the townspeople would have forgotten him entirely if they hadn't periodically seen the giant white horse, stamping and chomping and looking quite drowsy, at the hitching post.

Then, at nine A.M. on a Monday, the little man swept the sidewalk and with considerable ceremony hung up a mysterious sign that read SHADOWMAKER. Written in soap on the shop windows were the words GRAND OPENING.

The townspeople were puzzled over what exactly a shadowmaker was. When they went into his shop, there was nothing inside to price or appraise, nothing at all on the empty floor but the big, black trunk and a witch's broom.

"Er, perhaps we've come too early," a candy maker remarked.

"You call this a Grand Opening?" a grocer exclaimed. "Your shelves are empty, your showcases aren't filled, and you're not even playing any silly background music!"

The little man merely sat atop the big, black trunk, swinging his legs and tinkering with his crooked pipe. He said, "Actually, I'm overstocked. It only looks like I've run out of stuff to sell because what I sell is . . . shadows."

"Shadows?" asked the mayor.

"Shadows," the little man replied, putting the

pipe in his mouth. "Just what you've always needed."

"Shadows?" said the mayor a second time, no doubt hoping the little man's answer would change.

But it didn't. The Shadowmaker nodded and jumped off the black trunk and scurried about it with a bunch of keys on a ring, opening locks and throwing off chains. "I replace old shadows with new ones, plump shadows with lean ones, shabby shadows with spiffy ones that'll look more like the *real* you. Give me a trade-in and I'll give you a bargain. Cash only. One size fits all. Dressing rooms to your right. And—I don't accept returns."

The townspeople laughed or scratched their noggins or exchanged mocking glances. But the little man rolled up his right sleeve and reached down into the trunk. He fished around until he'd caught ahold of something and then yanked high the growling shadow of a wolf.

"Good heavens!" a woman shouted.

A man leapt away and screamed, "Yikes!"

"Aw, don't be such scaredy-cats," the little man said. "You're looking at a guy who's got everything under control."

It took the Shadowmaker the better part of an hour to show his entire collection. He lifted each shadow and turned it from side to side as if it were a mink coat or a rare museum piece. Meanwhile his customers uttered appreciative noises, like "Ooh!" and "Ah!" and "Zowie!"

What shadows did he show them? Those of a rooster, an airplane, a huge roller skate, a princess on a pogo stick, a plump chef flipping pancakes. The Shadowmaker pulled a giant dinosaur

shadow across the room and had to ask eight men to help him get it back into the trunk again. He even put a girl inside a sailboat shadow, but she got a little seasick. Finally he scooped out a snow-man shadow that left a chill in the air.

The Shadowmaker, wearied by all his heaving and hauling, collapsed on a stool to rest. The townspeople studied their own rather commonplace shadows, which lolled around their shoes like woebegone mud puddles. When the Shadowmaker thought they'd had enough time to consider their general scruffiness, he removed an order form from his greatcoat and said, "Okay, who's first and what'll it be?"

The mayor traded in his rumpled politician's shadow that he'd never been overly fond of and was soon parading down the street with the shadow of a grand king who wore a grand crown and sword and flowing cape. Then the other townspeople turned over their shadows and shivered as the little man stitched to their feet the shadow of a circus clown, say, or a rodeo cow-boy, or a pirate with a peg leg.

The Shadowmaker's business boomed. All afternoon customers rushed to his shop, exchanged careworn shadows for newfangled ones, and then walked about the town looking down at the sunlit sidewalks with satisfaction and vanity.

Chubby boys abruptly seemed skinny. Clumsy girls seemed nimble. Little children could rage and stomp like gruesome monsters—or at least their shadows could. A glad barber stood in the sun with a walrus beautifully sewn to his toes, a girl in the second grade wore the broad wings of an angel (a birthday gift from a loving aunt), and those unhappy people who were renting apartments where no pets were allowed now petted the shadows of puppies and kittens.

Nearly everyone was completely happy.

2

THE Shadowmaker's entire supply soon was sold out. The little man put up a sign that said TOUGH LUCK. TRY ME LATER. And all that night the Shadowmaker worked in absolute secrecy, making up more shadows.

However, someone was spying on him as he went into and came out of his shop, but the Shadowmaker never noticed. An ear was pressed to the shop door as he made frying sounds and snipped at something with scissors, but he never had a clue about that either.

The spy was a girl named Drizzle. She was nine years old and an orphan. She lived in a tin

shack across the railroad tracks with her penniless and cranky older brother, Soot. Drizzle was
a smart, pretty, good-hearted girl who loved her
brother dearly, even though he sometimes ig-
nored her, regularly raged at her, and persis-
tently untied her apron strings when she stood at
the stove.

Soot was thirteen years old and earned the
little money they had by repairing appliances,
lawn mowers, and outboard motors. He also
played dirty tricks on children. He would snatch
arithmetic homework from them or paint Ta-
basco sauce on postage stamps before they were
licked. He would creep under kitchen tables and
knot their shoelaces to the kitchen chairs. And
whenever children asked for butter at picnics,
he'd shove it into their thumbs.

The children hated him like poison and gave
him the nickname Soot because he was so nasty.
But his little sister was called Drizzle because

that was the name Soot had given her when he was once screaming at her and stamping his feet and saying things he didn't mean.

Soot had yelled, "You're Little Miss Sunshine to everybody! Everybody loves you! And that just shows they don't know you like I do! To me you're as gray as a rainy day. And your silly smiles are oozy! You're Drizzle to me. You're damp and you're dull! I wish you'd go away!"

His sister had wept at that—who wouldn't?—but Soot had only pointed at her tears and in triumph cried, "More drizzle! Drizzle's your name and Drizzle you'll stay, or I'm not Soot, your mean brother!"

You might guess it was hard for a sister to love a thirteen-year-old brother like Soot, but somehow Drizzle did. Each day on her way to school, Drizzle paused by a wishing well and dropped a stone or a cinder into its magical waters (she was too poor to drop pennies). Then she'd squint her eyes closed and wish, "May my brother's appliance, lawn mower, and outboard motor repair shop somehow make a go of it." Often she'd add as an afterthought, "And if you could make him a little less mean and grouchy, that would be very nice too."

So far the wishing well hadn't worked. Most people in the town were so prosperous they never had anything fixed. They simply threw things away and bought replacements. Or, if their lawn mowers, for example, were on the fritz, they kicked the engines and muttered "Drat" and rented goats to chew the grass. As a consequence Soot became more crabby and scared more customers away, and that made him angrier still. Now even spiders and roaches and rats slunk away from him.

Therefore, when news came to Drizzle about the hugely successful grand opening of the Shadowmaker's shop, she decided to spy on the little man in order to learn the tricks of his trade.

Perhaps she could get poor, unhappy Soot into the shadowmaking business too.

Each night she listened for her brother's snores and for the rustle of spiders and roaches and rats creeping back inside the tin shack. Then she sneaked out and crossed the railroad tracks and scooted down menacing dark alleys until she reached the loading dock of the Shadowmaker's shop, where the giant white horse drowsed beside a red coach that was like nothing she'd ever seen before.

Each night it was the same. She'd peek through the shop door's keyhole and see nothing but smoke and cans of black paint and the Shadowmaker reading a big purple book at the crate he used for a desk. Sometimes he would croon as he worked, and sometimes he would laugh "Tee hee." But more often he would shout, with gusto, rhymes that made no sense at all. "Alaska! Nebraska! Who asked ya?" was one. "Cow licks! Fort Dix! Raspberry pancake mix!" was another. And if the Shadowmaker was feeling frisky, he might add a "Sis boom bah!"

It was all very cheery and quaint, but it was not at all what Drizzle needed to know.

Sales continued to be brisk at the Shadowmaker's shop. Prior to the little man's arrival, no one in town had realized how puny and paltry and totally unlike themselves their miserable shadows were. But now that the little man had come, husbands and wives who'd splurged at the shop could look at each other's shadows with new affection. The Shadowmaker's black images brought romance back to the marriage. Or a grandmother who lived alone could fill her home with the shadows of her many grandchildren. Or little girls who were plagued with nightmares could lean the shadows of snarling dogs next to their windows and closet doors to keep the boogeyman out.

In no time at all the Shadowmaker became the richest man in town and his shop the busiest, though you couldn't tell by its shadow because it looked like the shadow of what it was—just a shop. The shadows of all the other places were palm trees or castles or spaceships—or a giant crown if the business was run by a man named King, or a colossal spoon and fork and plate if the place served customers dinner.

In no time at all, the sidewalks and streets were so covered with shadows that sundials couldn't give the time of day anymore, flowers had started to wilt, electricity bills were climbing, and the children went to and from school each day with flashlights. It seemed it was nighttime even at noon. And at night the moon and stars couldn't even be seen. Matters were, to say the very least, getting out of hand.

And Drizzle was getting slightly jealous. Her girlfriends had closets so jam-packed with shadows that their leopards and wood sprites were getting wrinkled. Drizzle, however, was still penniless and couldn't even pay for the shadow of a gerbil. As Drizzle looked down at the black puddle at her feet, she would pity herself and say, "Some girls' shadows look like princesses'; *my* shadow only looks like underpants that have dropped."

Drizzle wasn't the only one who was sighing. Soot was growlier than ever. Leaves curled on their branches when Soot slouched past, and wallpaper peeled in the room when he muttered and fumed and mourned their pathetic condition. He said, "Look at those happy people, Drizzle. Don't they burn you up? How come we've got to be so poor? How come we're at the end of our rope? How come it's you and me the children hate like poison?"

"Excuse me for interrupting, Soot," Soot's sister said. "You're right on the money about us being poor and at the end of our rope. But as for that last part, it's only *you* they hate like poison."

Soot gave Drizzle a mopey look and said, "And you wonder why I'm so pesky."

Drizzle hadn't given up on her scheme to pick up the Shadowmaker's tricks, but she was a little droopy over the results of her spying—she had, after all, learned zilch—so she continued with the wishing well even though Soot said that was goofy.

She took to heaving down the wishing well

bricks and boulders, hobnailed boots and mule harnesses, manhole covers and engine blocks.

She wished, "May Soot's repair shop get off the skids." "May Soot pull himself up by his bootstraps." "May Soot find a new lease on life." And so on.

Sometimes she would be a quarter mile away before she remembered what else she'd forgotten to wish. She would sock her forehead and rush back to the well and lean over the side to recite with a pant, "And if you could make him a little less grouchy, that would be very nice too."

Drizzle was worn to a frazzle. She was down in the dumps. She was about as blue as she could be. And then, as so often happens, just when Drizzle's world looked bleakest, certain events occurred that changed things for the better.

3

LATE one evening Drizzle was trying to cheer herself up by playing the trombone. She wasn't very accomplished on the instrument, and her music was, let's face it, just awful. She hadn't even completed one musical scale before her brother tramped into the room and said, "Why don't you play something you know?"

"That *was* something I know," replied Drizzle.

"Then why don't you shut off that terrible noise and let me pout in peace? Can't you see I've been down on my luck all day?"

Drizzle put down her trombone and smiled up

at Soot. "Maybe I'll just sit here and swing my legs and hum sweetly until you fall asleep."

Her brother regarded her suspiciously but went out, smacking his shoulder against the doorjamb. He complained all the way to his room. In spite of that, he was snoring almost as soon as he sank down on his mattress.

Drizzle got up and put her ear to his door. Then she skipped past the spiders that were creeping back into the shack and stole away to the Shadowmaker's shop.

She arrived earlier than usual, and what she saw was notably different. An orange cat sat licking its paws where the giant white horse had drowsed on other occasions. The red coach's windows were unshuttered, and inside it she could see brooms and wands and bullfrogs and bats, a dunce cap with gold stars on it, a smoking cauldron on a stove, and a grimy chemistry set. But the most important discovery was that the Shadowmaker's shop door was ajar an inch or so, beckoning Drizzle closer, an invitation she couldn't resist.

Drizzle climbed onto the loading dock and crawled close to the crack. She saw the Shadowmaker tinkering with a crooked pipe that wouldn't stay lit. He walked to a corner of the room that she couldn't see and then there was an unmistakable sizzle, the smell of cooking butter, and the Shadowmaker shouting, "Orange blossom! Play possum! Gonna cost 'em plenty!"

Drizzle's curiosity wouldn't keep. It lured her inside the shop's doorway just as the Shadowmaker yelled, "Sis boom bah!"

Suddenly the shop door slammed shut, swatting Drizzle inside. Party horns tooted, sleigh bells jingled, overhead lights blinked on and off, and giant cardboard hands with pointed fingers dropped from the ceiling and dangled accusingly near her face.

"Oh!" Drizzle said, rubbing her seat.

The Shadowmaker spun around, spewing

ashes from his pipe. "Wazzat?" the little man screeched. "Who's there?" he cried out as he made an effort to hide his cooking by spreading his greatcoat wide. He chewed nervously on his pipe stem as Drizzle stood up and brushed off her knees.

"I'm sorry about all the ruckus," she said. "It was rude of me to sneak in here."

The Shadowmaker grumbled in agreement as he lifted his greatcoat like wings and looked over his shoulder with worry.

"But if I were a burglar," Drizzle continued, "I surely wouldn't come here. All you have are a few yucky tools and cans of black paint and that griddle that's behind your coat."

The Shadowmaker winced when she said the word "griddle." Realizing that he had little left to camouflage, he let the sides of his greatcoat fall and said, "Little Miss Know-it-all, is it?"

"You must be thinking of someone else. Everyone calls me Drizzle." She saw that some-

thing was beginning to char on the griddle, but she didn't mention it.

The orange cat hopped up onto the windowsill and then poured itself down to the shop floor. The Shadowmaker was angrily scraping the griddle with a putty knife. *"Drizzle?"* he asked. "What kind of silly name is that?"

"Well, my father was Scandinavian, and my mother was—"

"Never mind that!" the little man said in his piercing voice. "Explain why you're snooping around here!"

Drizzle explained. "I hoped I could learn how you make shadows. Then maybe my brother could learn to make shadows too and pull himself up by his bootstraps, find a new lease on life, and—"

"Get off the skids?" the Shadowmaker asked.

"Why, yes!" Drizzle said with surprise.

The little man nodded. "I know the type."

"So you'll show me?"

"Nope," he said. "Nothing doing. I've got a crackerjack business now and I don't want any competition."

"But I've thought all that out!" Drizzle insisted. "You could move on to another town! You could open a chain of Shadowmaker shops! Hundreds of them nationwide! You could be even richer!"

The Shadowmaker struck a match off the orange cat's chin and waved the match over his pipe bowl. He said, "You're a cagey one, aren't you?"

"Uh-huh," Drizzle said, for she was nothing if not truthful. "And I'm also pretty and good-hearted and I love my older brother, Soot, even though he's cranky and penniless and plays mean tricks on children."

The Shadowmaker wasn't paying attention. He lifted his big rubber boots and looked under

his coat and squinted into the room's four cor-
ners. "Did I just strike a match off a cat's chin?"

"Yes."

The Shadowmaker looked at Drizzle in shock.
"Then whatever you do, don't sneeze!"

4

UNTIL the Shadowmaker suggested it, Drizzle hadn't an inkling that a sneeze was coming on, but no sooner were the words out of his mouth than her nose started to tickle. And before she could find the hankie in her pocket, Drizzle sneezed—not noisily, not with zeal, but with a dainty, dinky sound like *"kitchen."*

Yet that was more than enough to somehow transform the orange cat into a huge green dragon. Aside from the fire coming out of its jagged mouth and its general ugliness, it really didn't seem like such a wicked or worrisome monster to Drizzle. It simply seemed startled to be a dragon and crowding them in that room.

But the Shadowmaker was rattled. He raced about opening boxes and suitcases and metal cabinet doors, wailing, "Where are my bangers?"

"Your what?" Drizzle asked.

The little man looked over his shoulder and saw the green dragon flick its forked tongue out

like a hungry and overlarge lizard. He went white and cried, "Sneeze again!"

"I can't."

"Then fake it!" he screamed as he shook out a wastepaper basket that seemed to contain no bangers.

"Kitchen," she said obediently. The dragon abruptly became a calm sea turtle that blinked as though it were getting sleepy. Astonished by her trick, Drizzle said *"kitchen"* again, and this time the sea turtle turned into a horrible creature all covered in wild grass and slime, with great claws and a yellow beak and long, clashing teeth. The creature roared like a tractor and made the shop walls quiver like jelly. Then it stalked toward Drizzle as she cowered, speechless.

At last the Shadowmaker unearthed his bangers—two garbage can lids—and clapped them together with an earsplitting clang. The giant white horse was suddenly there in the room, looking relaxed and slow-witted and drowsy.

"Phew!" said Drizzle.

The Shadowmaker frowned at her. "This kind of aggravation I don't need."

"You're a wizard, huh?"

"You don't miss a trick, do you?"

"That's how you make shadows. You wizard them."

The little man eyed Drizzle and took off his gray bowler hat. He wore a wizard beanie under it. He said, "You're not going to spill the beans on me, are you?"

Drizzle licked a tooth as she looked at him. "I thought wizards lived in swamps or on mountain-tops and spent their days wrestling with the dastardly forces of evil."

The Shadowmaker sat down on a stool and looked at the girl from under the awnings of his black eyebrows. "You're thinking of your hot-shot wizards, your prizewinners. Me, I'm strictly second-rate, minor league, semipro. I'm playing way over my head right now." His voice lowered and he looked to the right and left before he confessed, "A great wizard doesn't use garbage can lids."

"Still, I'll bet the people in town will be

pleased to know even a second-rate wizard's around.''

The Shadowmaker hopped up from the stool. ''Oh, sure. And then they'll be asking me for favors: fix this, mend that, make this work again.'' He clanged together the bangers and the giant white horse lost the antlers that it was starting to grow.

''You don't have to worry about people asking you to fix or mend anything around here,'' said Drizzle. ''Ask my brother, Soot. He's a repairman and we're penniless. The townspeople here simply buy new things or kick their engines and say 'Drat!' ''

The Shadowmaker's eyebrows lifted. ''Your brother's a repairman?''

''Why, yes,'' said Drizzle. ''He can make broken things work just like they're brand-new.'' She lowered her eyes in sorrow. ''But he's down on his luck just now.''

''We've been through that.''

"Oh. I forgot."

The Shadowmaker scratched his beard and chomped on his crooked pipe. Then he said, "I'll tell you what, Drizzle. You can't just start up a shop like this at the drop of a hat. I mean, shadowmaking's a science! You need permits, licenses, years of experience. And you need the recipe."

"I'll be happy to pay you for it."

"You said you were penniless."

Drizzle gave it some thought. She said, "Maybe I could teach you how to play the trombone and pay you off that way."

"You got a deal," the Shadowmaker said, and clapped his hands around hers.

"You'll give me the recipe?"

"You betcha. I'll come by for you next Friday and turn over the shop, the secret recipe, the whole kit and caboodle." The Shadowmaker dug deep into his greatcoat pocket and took out a rusty penny. "Here, take this for your trouble.

And don't say a peep to anyone about who I am."

"A *penny?*" she said. "Don't say a peep for a measly penny?"

"Hey, even a shadow of an elephant—which is, if I say so myself, a jim-dandy piece of work and a very hot item around here—even that's small potatoes compared to that lucky penny."

"Gosh, this has all been so easy!"

The Shadowmaker smiled. "Your ship's come

in. You and your repairman brother are gonna hear opportunity knock at your door.''

"And pennies will come down like raindrops, I'll bet.''

The Shadowmaker winked at her. "Hey, now you're talking.''

"But—"

"I'll come for you next Friday.''

Drizzle skipped back toward the tin shack she called home, feeling giddy and optimistic. The penny, as lucky pennies will, seemed to heat whichever fist she put it in. As she skipped past the wishing well, something in the air seemed to clutch her wrist and yank her rudely off her feet. She bounced twice and then was dragged by the penny until she smacked against the wishing well's cold, damp stones. She could hear the magical waters tumbling and boiling below, and scents like cinnamon and ginger nicely teased her nose.

Drizzle leaned over into the wishing well and yelled down, "You know, if I weren't so wise beyond my years, I'd think you were trying to get me to throw my lucky penny away."

A great rumbling and scalding noise rose up from the depths, and Drizzle leapt backward in surprise. Then she remembered that pennies weren't lucky unless you gave them to someone else. Drizzle said, "Easy come, easy go," and flipped the coin over her shoulder.

The magical waters first made a sound like *"Glup!"* and then a satisfied *"Yessss!"*

Drizzle bent excitedly over the stone wall and asked, "Does that mean I get my wish?"

"Galump," said the wishing well.

"You mean my brother's appliance, lawn mower, and outboard motor repair shop will somehow make a go of it?"

"Piddaloop."

"And Soot will pull himself up by his bootstraps?"

The wishing well replied, *"Billabup."*

"Thanks," said Drizzle. Then she heard the wishing well say, "The pleasure was all mine"— in its own language, of course.

By the time Drizzle got home, she was so contented with her night's work that she forgot Soot was sleeping and let the screen door slap shut.

"Drizzle!" Soot called out. "Drizzle, is that you?"

She ran to a chair and perched on it and said, "Yes, brother dear. It's your little good-hearted sister, Drizzle. I've just been sitting here swinging my legs and humming sweetly. And it's not as late as the clock says it is."

His bedsprings creaked, and the floorboards boomed and the shack windows rattled as Soot clomped out. Drizzle cringed, thinking he might squirt water at her or dangle a mouse in front of her nose.

But her brother merely sagged haggardly

against the doorframe, looking sorry and unkempt, his hair as wild as marsh weeds. "You woke me up from the scariest nightmare," said Soot. "A real lulu. I was in the yard with all that junk out there; nothing else but junk. And you were missing. I looked for you but couldn't find you. I looked and looked and looked everywhere. I was scared you'd run away. I was yelling, 'Drizzle! Drizzle, come back! I'll be good to you, Drizzle! I'll make amends! Just please come back!'" Soot paused and looked at her sheepishly. "I was crying," he said. "I was crying real hard. I thought maybe putting those strings in your spaghetti last night might've been the last straw; that maybe you'd gone for good."

Drizzle said, "I'd cry too—if I thought you had run away."

"Yeah?" Soot grinned and gave himself height. He coughed in order to get up his nerve and then admitted, "I love you, Drizzle. You're my sister so I don't say it enough, but I really love and appreciate you." Soot wiped his mouth with embarrassment and picked at his pajama cuff as he said, "I gotta get it off my chest: I'm sorry I spit those watermelon seeds at you yesterday."

"And the syrup?" she asked.

"I owe you an apology for that too," Soot agreed. "How'd you ever get the book open again?"

"And the tadpoles in my soup? You're sorry for that too?"

"Yep. I gotta make peace with you, Drizzle. That nightmare really walloped me."

Drizzle didn't speak.

Soot dropped to his knees and appealed to her. "Please say you'll forgive me!"

Drizzle couldn't say it just then. She was thinking about the lucky penny and the wishing well and how her ship was coming in just like the little man had said it would. Drizzle sugared her voice to say, "I'll forgive you if you promise me you'll change your attitudes."

Her brother gave her the fisheye. "How?"

"First: No more moping around and wallowing in self-pity."

"Okay."

"Second: Stop feeling so down on your luck."

Soot gave it some thought and said, "Done."

"And go with me to someplace in a week."

"Which place?"

"Just say you will."

Her brother shrugged. "I will."

"Oh joy!" Drizzle cried out, both because it was joy that she felt and because there's a rule that heroines must cry out "Oh joy!" at least once in their lives, and she thought it wise to get the silly obligation over with.

5

JOY stayed with Drizzle and Soot through the next morning and the next several days. But joy was not with the Shadowmaker. The Shadowmaker experienced a wretched morning, a worse afternoon, and days that had him pounding his fists and screaming, "Alack!"

His problems were caused by the shadows he had sold. His shadows were now acting haywire.

The mayor's grand royal shadow had developed an annoying squeak in its knee, its crown kept tipping off to one side, and its luxurious cape kept unfastening.

An engineer complained to the Shadowmaker that his shadow of a locomotive was just right

when he was in a big room, like a church or a courthouse, but whenever he went into his bathroom his shadow would clang against the bathtub with an earsplitting *gong.*

The grocer's wife wept that she missed her old shadow and the cute way it had of bending when she passed a wall or crinkling when she walked up the stairs. She claimed the swan shadow she'd bought squashed against the bottom step and didn't budge as she climbed up or would show only its twiggy legs when she stood too close to a wall. Plus it seemed she was spending half her day ironing out its graceful neck.

The Shadowmaker's products, the townspeople discovered, just weren't as good as their original shadows. His shadows always seemed to need silencing or pressing or cheering up. When it was cold, the shadows of dresses were so stiff that the dancers made a clunking noise as they glided across the ballroom. When it was hot, the shadow of an igloo melted and a shopkeeper was forced to close his appliance store just to mop up the black mess.

Everyone began to be grumpy and angry and sorry that the Shadowmaker had happened on their town. They needed shadows in good working order like they'd never needed working doorbells or toasters or outboard motors. Now they crowded into the Shadowmaker's shop yelling to get their old shadows back—or at least get their new shadows repaired.

The Shadowmaker made excuses and wrote out repair estimates on a clipboard. He put off the owners by saying that the soonest he could get to their shadows would be in about a week. And as the week wore on, the Shadowmaker said he had another grand opening coming up in a couple of days. And when Thursday came he said he had a great deal to do the next day, but stop by on Saturday and he could fix up the shadow in a jiffy.

As it happened, all the townspeople ended up

with appointments on Saturday, but only Drizzle knew that. Drizzle collected every scrap of news and rumor about the Shadowmaker, but she never said a peep about him being a wizard—and a second-rate, minor-league wizard at that, a little man who was not at all in control of his inventions. And she didn't say a word to anyone, not even Soot, about the little man's promise of the secret recipe. She merely passed the time playing the trombone and patiently waited to hear opportunity knocking at the door.

6

BUT opportunity didn't knock. Friday night came and the workweek ended and the Shadowmaker never showed up at the tin shack as he had promised he would. By nine o'clock Drizzle was steamed, and she marched into Soot's room. "You remember me saying I wanted you to go with me someplace?"

"Are we going?" Soot asked.

"Get your shoes on."

And that's how it was that Soot and Drizzle ran out of the shack and crossed the railroad tracks and scooted down menacing alleys until they got to the Shadowmaker's shop. His giant white horse was harnessed to the red coach, which was backed up to the loading dock so that the little man could shove his griddle and crate and tools inside.

"Looks like he's busy," said Soot.

"He's more than busy," Drizzle said. "He's about to fly the coop!" Drizzle stomped forward and put her fists on her hips like a shrew as she yelled, "And what, may I ask, is the meaning of this?"

The Shadowmaker flinched and then falsely smiled at the girl. "Oh, there you are, Drizzle! I've been looking high and low for you!"

"I'll just bet you've been," she said in a voice that smoked with anger.

"And this must be Soot."

Soot waved slightly and asked, "How ya doing?"

The Shadowmaker didn't reply. He was justifying himself to Drizzle by saying, "Honest. I was going to stop by your shack on my way out."

"It's not *on* your way."

"Isn't it? I got the wrong directions, I guess. Anyway, sooner or later I was going to look you up and chat about what a swell time it's been and how I'm gonna miss those zany moments we've had together." He winked at Soot. "Your sister's great."

"Yep," the boy said. "She can be a lotta laughs."

Drizzle said, "You were supposed to give me the recipe and get Soot off the skids!"

"And did I?" the Shadowmaker asked.

"No."

The Shadowmaker sucked a match flame into his pipe tobacco and went back to his moving chores. "Then I lied."

Drizzle was beside herself. She clambered onto the dock and pursued the little man inside. "But that's not nice! That's worse than not nice—it's *lousy*!"

The Shadowmaker sat on the black trunk and crossed his little legs. "Hey, you want lousy, take a peek at my shadows. Sheez, did I goof up with those!" The Shadowmaker sucked on his pipe but couldn't draw any smoke. "I must've been daydreaming in wizard school. I should've paid closer attention."

Soot walked into the shop as though he had nothing better to do and immediately began tinkering with a clock that wasn't working.

Drizzle said reasonably, "You could at least give back the original shadows before you light out of town."

The Shadowmaker reddened and scanned his big rubber boots. "Well, that's something else I sort of botched." His right eyebrow lifted so that his blue eye could see Drizzle's doubt and fury. "You don't believe me?" The Shadowmaker jumped down from the trunk and strained at its lid until it crashed back. "Peek inside," he said.

Drizzle stared into a cavern that seemed to be without bottom, that seemed deeper than outer space. It was as dark as night on Halloween, so

black that the shop's candle flames were pulled
to it and Drizzle's nose was becoming frostbit-
ten. She could feel her shoes moving forward
inch by inch but couldn't imagine what was tug-
ging them. And then she spilled over backward
as her shadow was ripped out from under her
and yanked into the trunk like a rug.

The Shadowmaker slammed the lid down in
the nick of time and it smashed on her shadow's
wriggling ankles. Soot joined them in wrenching
and jerking until Drizzle's shadow was loose
from the pull of the mixed-up shadows inside. As
the Shadowmaker sewed it back on her, he said,
"You can see what my problem is, can't you,
Drizzle? I'll never sort those shadows out. It's
pandemonium in there."

The Shadowmaker worked at plowing the
black trunk toward the coach as Soot put a spring
inside the clock and screwed it back together.
Soot asked, "Can't you fix up the shadows you
sold everyone?"

"Oh, I can repair them," the little man said. "At least I know *how* to. But I'm pretty stupid with tools, and if I stuck around I'd be swamped with work and wouldn't have any time for mixing potions and such." He shut the red coach's rear doors, locked them, and scuttled down from the loading dock.

The Shadowmaker had forgotten his bangers. Drizzle got the garbage can lids and secretly buttoned her coat over them. Then she skipped down the stairs after the little man, making an effort not to clatter. "But Soot *loves* that sort of thing," Drizzle said. "He's an appliance, lawn mower, and outboard motor repairman, remember?"

Soot waggled the clock he'd been tinkering with by his ear and grinned at his sister. "Got her ticking again!"

"See?" Drizzle said. "You could show him how to repair shadows and Soot could run your shop while you made it rain or turned frogs into princes or did whatever it is you're good at."

The Shadowmaker scrambled up a ladder and into the driver's seat and hung his gray bowler hat on the brake after he released it. "Nah, I think I'd rather fly the coop and maybe come back to this town in a year or two. They'll be neck-high in the goofy shadows by then. They'll forget it was me who got it all started and they'll pay through the nose to get things straight again."

Drizzle looked at her brother. "Have you ever seen such a nasty little scoundrel?"

Soot was adjusting the hands on the clock to get them to the right time. He said, "The guy's just like *I* used to be—before I decided to get off the skids."

The Shadowmaker chucked his giant white horse and the red coach rolled forward, cinders crunching under its wheels. He yelled over his shoulder, "When it's night in your rooms with the lights on and the only color you know is black and it's cold as winter even in August, I'll be right around the corner!"

His exit seemed so mean that Drizzle wanted to spit and say "Hooey!" Instead she sank down by the dock in despair, and Soot walked over to pet back her hair. "You tried your best," he said.

She looked up at him with tears in her eyes,

but then the bangers clanked under her coat and she realized what she could still do. She stood up and cupped her hands around her mouth and screamed, "Kitchen!" and the giant white horse became a yawning hippopotamus.

"What's this?" the Shadowmaker cried, though he was wizard enough to know. "What sort of shenanigans are you up to?"

"Kitchen!" Drizzle yelled again, and much to her amazement the hippopotamus remained a hippopotamus but the red coach became a pirate ship.

The Shadowmaker was anxiously hunting for the garbage can lids, patting each of his greatcoat pockets, stirring his hand around inside a large suitcase. He looked to the loading dock and shouted hotly, "You've got my bangers, don't you?"

"Kitchen!" Drizzle yelled one more time, and the Shadowmaker's gray bowler hat turned into a pelican's nest.

Soot was simply looking on, more than puzzled. He said, "This is getting interesting."

"It's a chain reaction," the Shadowmaker cried. "I'm next! I'll go poof! I'll disappear! Whatever you do, don't sneeze!"

"Okay," Drizzle said. "I'll give your bangers back if you teach Soot how to mend shadows."

The Shadowmaker smirked and walked toward her, growing two feet taller with each step, growing purple hair all over. "I'll get those bangers back by hook or by crook!"

Drizzle presumed shape shifting was one of the easier wizard tricks, but as the Shadowmaker snarled and crossed his eyes and gave himself red devil wings, she sank down by the dock with Soot. She was getting pretty frightened. The Shadowmaker grew as big as a purple house, green smoke came out of his mouth and ears, and the ground shook as though it too was scared when the Shadowmaker growled, "I'll have those bangers, little girl, or I'll eat you up like a candy bar!"

Soot yelled, "Nobody talks to *my* sister that way!" And he jumped up and ran over and stamped on the Shadowmaker's huge toes.

"Argh!" the Shadowmaker howled. He grabbed Soot by one leg, jerked him upside down, and dangled the boy over his great open mouth as if he were about to eat pizza.

"Ki—" Drizzle said, and suddenly the Shadowmaker lost his grip on Soot. Her brother jumped free and said, "I owe ya one, Drizzle!" as the Shadowmaker plunked to the earth on his rump, a purple monster still, but a dizzy one. He wiped his eyes as if he'd just woken up. Then he crept fiendishly toward Drizzle.

"Kit—" Drizzle said and the Shadowmaker wailed. His elbows jerked up as if he were on puppet strings and his nose grew into a carrot. "I'll be turned into a boxing glove," he cried, "or a green parakeet, or a seed catalogue in South Dakota!"

"Kitch—" Drizzle said.

His ears became cookies, his hands telephones; his wizard beanie became an octopus pulling the skin of his head. The Shadowmaker began shrinking. He wept. He shuffled over to Drizzle on his knees as she got out the bangers. "Please, Drizzle!" he begged. "Clang them!" The Shadowmaker clasped his telephones together and pleaded, "Drizzle! I'll do anything!"

"Anything?" Drizzle asked.

7

So Drizzle clanged the bangers together and everything got straightened out. In no time at all there was just a giant white horse and red coach outside—no octopus or pelican's nest or pirate ship or hippo. The Shadowmaker and Soot huddled on the shop floor, reading blueprints, cooking recipes on the griddle, and snipping and sewing and hammering, rehearsing magic spells. The last thing Drizzle heard before she slipped into a cozy sleep was the Shadowmaker shouting, "Parsnips! Basketball! Minnesota tree!" and Soot shouting back, "Dictionary! Grease monkey! Lube jobs free!"

Drizzle awoke at sunrise and saw her brother

crouched on the shop floor, all cleaned up and spiffy. He was happily lettering a wood shingle that read, SHADOWMENDER.

The Shadowmaker had gone without a good-bye, taking his garbage can lids along with him. Drizzle was a little sad about his going, but not very, since Soot was so pleased with his new occupation.

Soot asked his sister, "You know what today is? Saturday! All the people in town have appointments to see me and get their shadows repaired! Just look." Soot pulled a drape aside and Drizzle saw hundreds of noses pressed against the shop window and eyes peering in. Customers were rapping on the shop door and jumping up and down with impatience and calling, "Open up!" or "Don't push!" Some had their shadows in shopping bags and some had their shadows on hangers. Some were wearing their shadows like black raincoats or droopy socks.

Soot was so pleased, he clapped his hands to-

gether and told his sister, "I can't wait." He cried out to the townspeople, "Okay! Opening up!" As soon as Soot unlocked the shop door, the townspeople spilled inside like a tipped-over package of doughnuts. Soot gave Drizzle a thumbs up and whispered to her, "Zowie!"

And the people in the town? Well, thanks to Drizzle they're completely happy again. They scarcely give the Shadowmaker a thought anymore, unless they happen to read a newspaper story about a city trapped inside pink bubble gum, or a town where women wear squids instead of hats, or a faraway land where children say "Spaghetti" and flap their arms and fly over the moon just like purple cows.